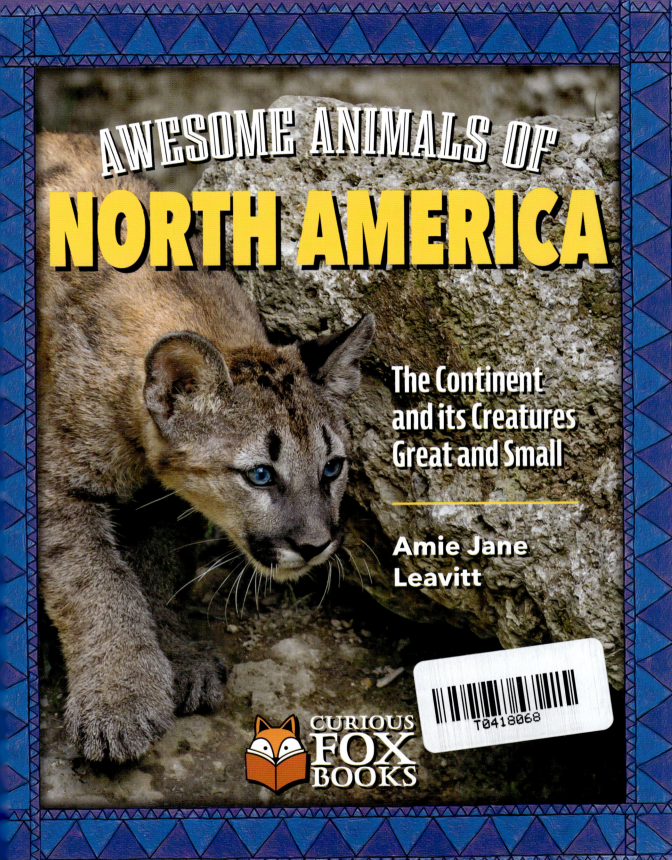

AWESOME ANIMALS OF NORTH AMERICA

The Continent and its Creatures Great and Small

Amie Jane Leavitt

CURIOUS FOX BOOKS

Banff (BAMF) National Park, shown here, is a beautiful forested area of Canada.

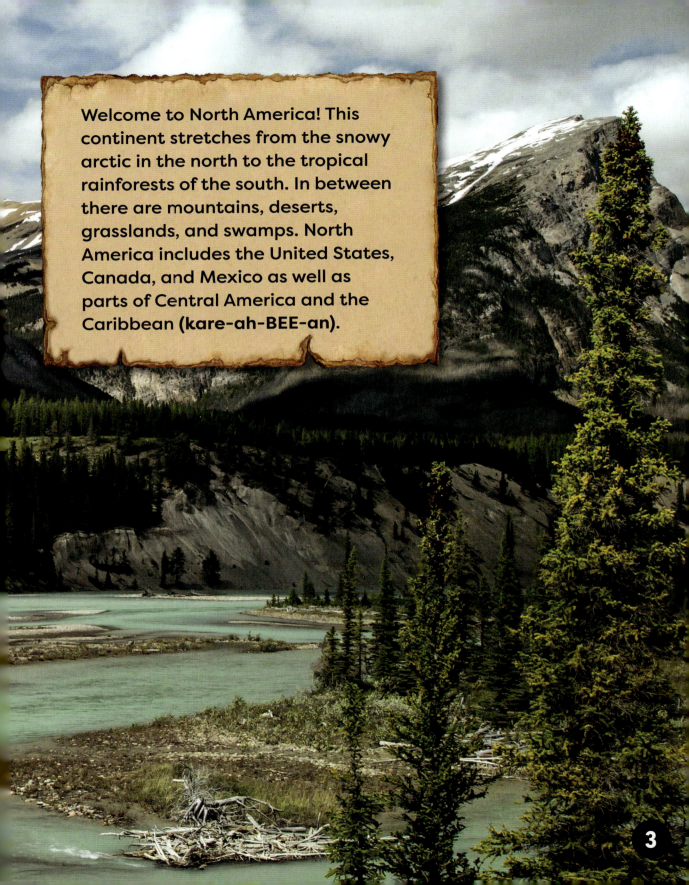

Welcome to North America! This continent stretches from the snowy arctic in the north to the tropical rainforests of the south. In between there are mountains, deserts, grasslands, and swamps. North America includes the United States, Canada, and Mexico as well as parts of Central America and the Caribbean (kare-ah-BEE-an).

GILA MONSTER
Length: 2 feet (61 centimeters), including tail
Weight: 5 pounds (2.2 kilograms)
Habitat: deserts of southwest US and Mexico
Diet: rodents, birds, reptiles, and eggs

The Gila (HEE-lah) monster is the biggest lizard in the North American desert. A desert is dry and home to many plants and animals. Gila monsters are venomous. They have a black body with yellow, orange, or pink patterns.

Jackrabbits also live in the desert. Heat leaves their bodies through their big ears, keeping them cool. Jackrabbits sprint up to 40 miles (64 kilometers) per hour.

JACKRABBIT
Length: 2 feet (61 centimeters)
Weight: 6 pounds (2.7 kilograms)
Habitat: scrublands of US and Mexico
Diet: grasses and leaves

PRAIRIE DOG

Length: 18 inches (46 centimeters), including tail
Weight: 3 pounds (1.4 kilograms)
Habitat: grasslands of central US
Diet: grasses and insects

Just northeast of the American desert are the Great Plains. Many kinds of animals live here. Prairie (PRAYR-ee) dogs burrow under the soil to create elaborate burrows. Close family groups share these tunnels, which are called dog towns. Prairie dogs get their name because they bark.

COUGAR

Length: 8 feet (2.4 meters), including tail
Weight: 160 pounds (73 kilograms)
Habitat: mountains, forests, deserts, and swamps of western North America
Diet: deer, sheep, small mammals, and birds

The cougar lives in a large range across North America. It has been seen and named by many people, which is why it is also known as a mountain lion or puma. Cougars cannot roar but make chirps and growls.

Coyotes are part of the dog family. They make a wide range of noises, including barks and howls. Because of their loud calls, they are sometimes called song dogs.

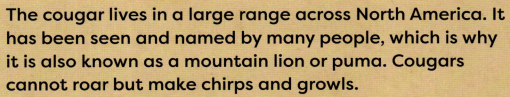

COYOTE

Length: 4½ feet (1.4 meters), including tail
Weight: 40 pounds (18 kilograms)
Habitat: grasslands, deserts, forests, and mountains of North America
Diet: deer, sheep, small mammals, birds, and reptiles

AMERICAN BISON
Length: 12 feet (3.7 meters)
Weight: 2,400 pounds (1,089 kilograms)
Habitat: grasslands of US and Canada
Diet: grasses

The American bison is the largest mammal in North America. Just like hippos, you shouldn't judge them on their size! Bison can run up to 35 miles (56 kilometers) per hour. The bison is sometimes called a buffalo, but that name actually belongs to a completely different animal!

BALD EAGLE

Wingspan: 8 feet (2.4 meters)
Weight: 12 pounds (5.4 kilograms)
Habitat: coasts and wetlands of North America
Diet: fish, rodents, and birds

The bald eagle is the United States' national bird. Born with all-brown feathers, it gets its head of white feathers by age five. Bald eagles make their large nests high in tall trees. The largest nest found was 9½ feet (3 meters) wide and 20 feet (6 meters) tall.

Soaring high above the trees at night is the great horned owl. This is the most common owl in North America. It has puffs of feathers on its head that look like horns.

GREAT HORNED OWL
Wingspan: 4½ feet (1.4 meters)
Weight: 3½ pounds (1.6 kilograms)
Habitat: forests, mountains, grasslands, and wetlands of North America
Diet: small mammals, birds, and reptiles

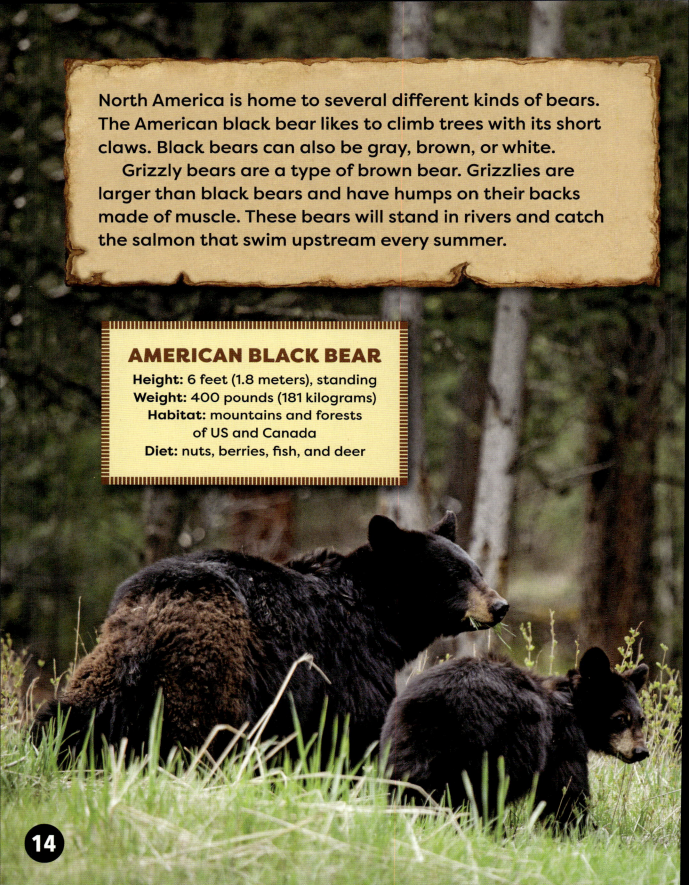

North America is home to several different kinds of bears. The American black bear likes to climb trees with its short claws. Black bears can also be gray, brown, or white.
Grizzly bears are a type of brown bear. Grizzlies are larger than black bears and have humps on their backs made of muscle. These bears will stand in rivers and catch the salmon that swim upstream every summer.

AMERICAN BLACK BEAR

Height: 6 feet (1.8 meters), standing
Weight: 400 pounds (181 kilograms)
Habitat: mountains and forests of US and Canada
Diet: nuts, berries, fish, and deer

GRIZZLY BEAR

Height: 8 feet (2.4 meters), standing
Weight: 900 pounds (408 kilograms)
Habitat: mountains and forests of northern US and Canada
Diet: nuts, berries, fish, and deer

POLAR BEAR
Height: 11 feet (3.4 meters), standing
Weight: 1,400 pounds (635 kilograms)
Habitat: tundra of North America
Diet: seals, caribous, birds, and fish

Polar bears live in North America's coldest habitat, the Arctic. Their thick fur is white because it's hollow. Their skin is actually black! The fur also reflects sunlight. This is how the polar bear stays so warm. A polar bear can swim for several days at a time.

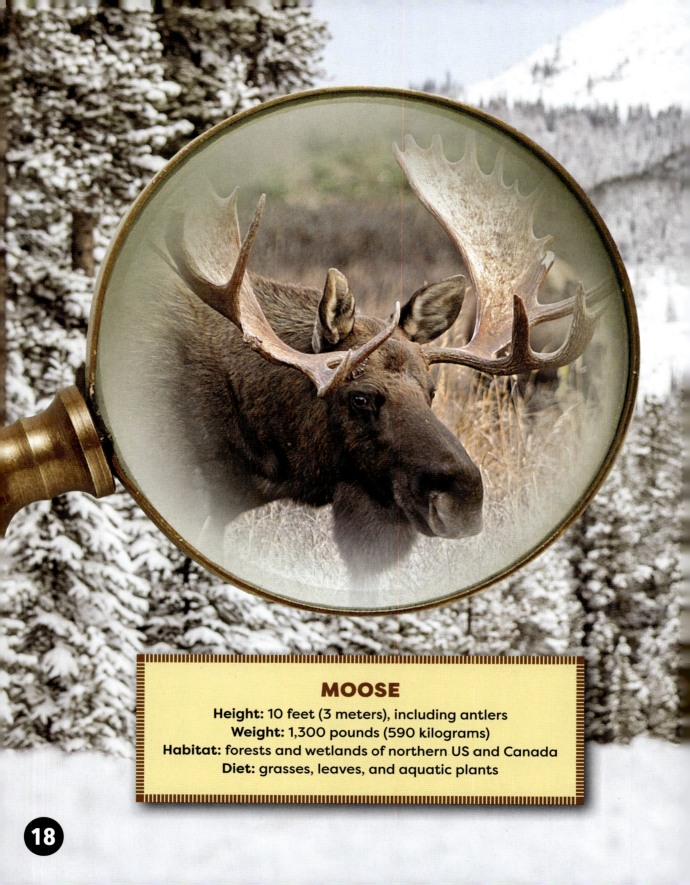

MOOSE

Height: 10 feet (3 meters), including antlers
Weight: 1,300 pounds (590 kilograms)
Habitat: forests and wetlands of northern US and Canada
Diet: grasses, leaves, and aquatic plants

Moose are huge animals. Their long legs keep their body above the snow, so they don't mind the cold. Moose antlers are used for fighting or defending. Moose shed their antlers every year.

AMERICAN ALLIGATOR
Length: 12 feet (3.7 meters)
Weight: 1,000 pounds (454 kilograms)
Habitat: wetlands of southeast US
Diet: deer, birds, and amphibians

The American alligator spends its days creeping along the waterways looking like a bumpy brown log. This helps it sneak up on its prey. The alligator's nose is turned upward so it can breathe when the rest of its body is hiding in the water.

Alligators make small ponds called alligator holes. These holes hold water during dry seasons and can be homes to other animals.

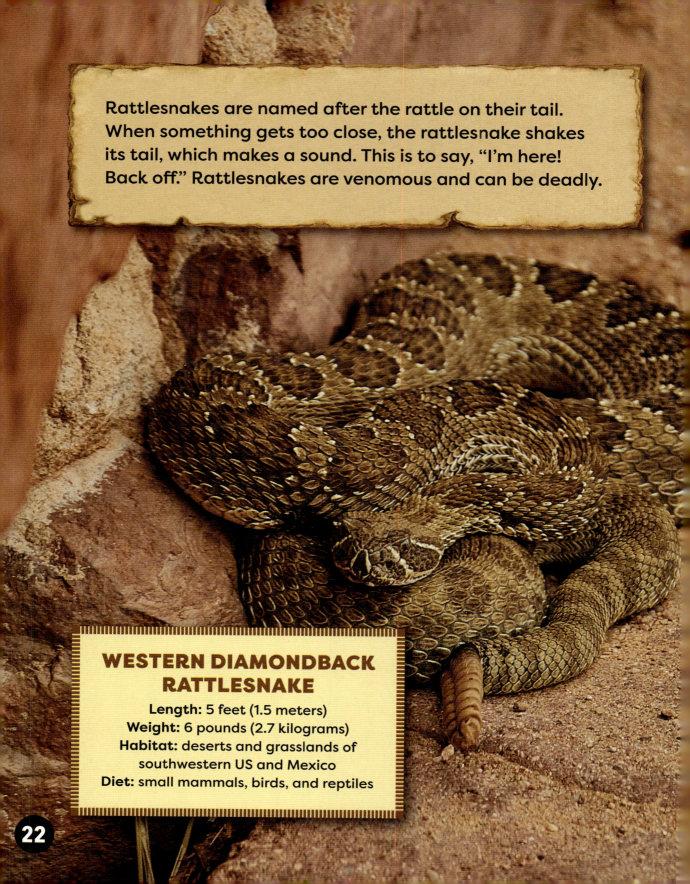

Rattlesnakes are named after the rattle on their tail. When something gets too close, the rattlesnake shakes its tail, which makes a sound. This is to say, "I'm here! Back off." Rattlesnakes are venomous and can be deadly.

WESTERN DIAMONDBACK RATTLESNAKE

Length: 5 feet (1.5 meters)
Weight: 6 pounds (2.7 kilograms)
Habitat: deserts and grasslands of southwestern US and Mexico
Diet: small mammals, birds, and reptiles

The cottonmouth snake likes to swim in bodies of water. It is venomous but rarely bites humans. Cottonmouths get their name because the inside of their mouths are white.

COTTONMOUTH
Length: 4 feet (1.2 meters)
Weight: 20 ounces (567 grams)
Habitat: wetlands of southeast US
Diet: fish, birds, small mammals, and amphibians

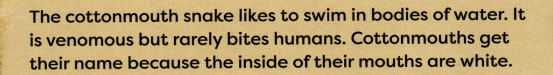

The resplendent quetzal (re-SPLEN-dent ket-SAWL) has shiny green feathers that look like the wet leaves of the rainforest. Male quetzals have tail feathers that grow to 39 inches (99 centimeters) long, almost three times their body length!

RESPLENDENT QUETZAL
Wingspan: 14 inches (36 centimeters)
Weight: 8 ounces (227 grams)
Habitat: rainforests of Mexico and Central America
Diet: fruits, insects, reptiles, and amphibians

The monarch butterfly spends summers in Canada, springs in the United States, and winters in central Mexico. Monarchs have the longest migration of any insect species.

MONARCH BUTTERFLY

Wingspan: 4 inches (10 centimeter)
Weight: 500 milligrams
Habitat: grasslands of North America
Diet: leaves and nectar

An axolotl (AX-oh-lot-ul) only lives in two lakes in the world, Lake Xochimilco (SOH-chee-mil-koh) and Lake Chalco (CHAL-koh). The feathery things around the axolotl's head are its gills. The axolotl lives underwater all its life and can swim up to 10 miles (16 kilometers) per hour.

AMERICAN LOBSTER
Length: 2 feet (61 centimeters)
Weight: 9 pounds (4.1 kilograms)
Habitat: Atlantic Coast of North America
Diet: mollusks, crabs, small fish, and algae

AXOLOTL
Length: 9 inches (23 centimeters)
Weight: 8 ounces (227 grams)
Habitat: lakes of Mexico
Diet: worms, insects, and small fish

Blue crabs are excellent swimmers. Their back legs work as paddles as they move through the water. American lobsters have 10 legs. They crawl on the ocean floor looking for food.

ATLANTIC BLUE CRAB
Width: 9 inches (23 centimeters)
Weight: 5 ounces (142 grams)
Habitat: Atlantic Coast of North America
Diet: mollusks, crabs, small fish, and algae

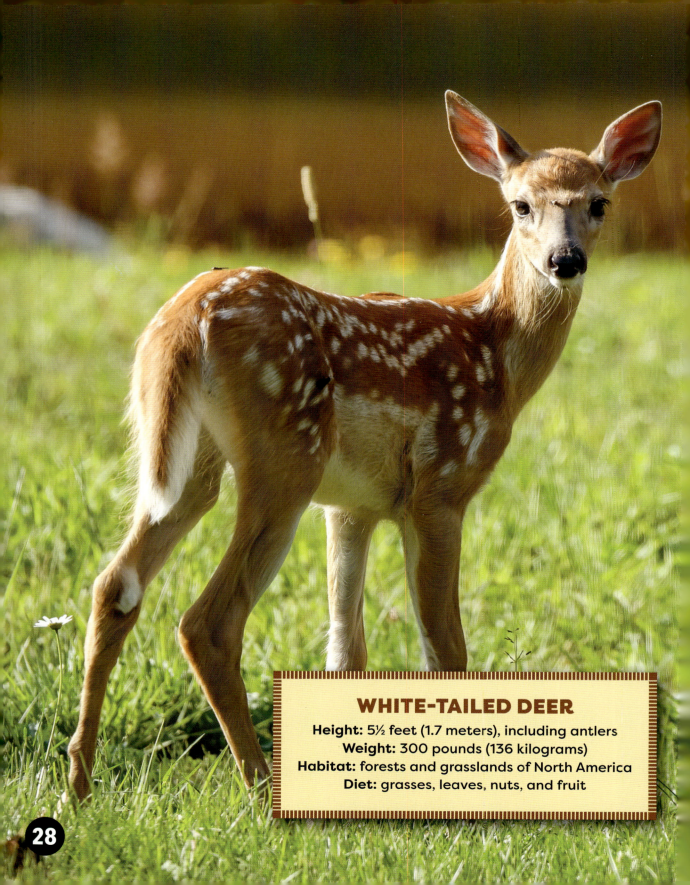

WHITE-TAILED DEER

Height: 5½ feet (1.7 meters), including antlers
Weight: 300 pounds (136 kilograms)
Habitat: forests and grasslands of North America
Diet: grasses, leaves, nuts, and fruit

The beaver builds its home, called a lodge, in North American streams. It swims in and out through an underwater entrance.

White-tailed deer will raise their tails when they sense danger. The bright white is easily noticed by other deer, and they are on alert to run away.

People travel all over North America. Everywhere they go, they find new animals to meet!

NORTH AMERICAN BEAVER

Length: 4 feet (1.2 meters), including tail
Weight: 44 pounds (20 kilograms)
Habitat: wetlands of North America
Diet: wood, leaves, and aquatic plants

FURTHER READING

Books

De Seve, Karen and Nancy Castaldo. *National Geographic Kids Mission: Polar Bear Rescue: All About Polar Bears and How to Save Them.* Washington, D.C.: NG Kids Mission: Animal Rescue, 2014.

Ganeri, Anita. *Gila Monster (A Day in the Life: Desert Animals).* New York: Heinemann, 2011.

George, Jean Craighead. *The Buffalo Are Back.* New York: Dutton Books for Young Readers, 2010.

Marsh, Laura. *Alligators and Crocodiles.* Washington, D.C.: National Geographic Kids, 2015.

Widman, William. *Owls For Kids: A Children's Book About Owls, Owl Facts, Life, and Pictures.* Amazon Digital Services, 2015.

Websites

Explore: Polar Bear Cam
    https://explore.org/livecams/polar-bears/polar-bear-cam
Active Wild: North American Animals
    https://www.activewild.com/north-american-animals
The San Diego Zoo: North America
    http://animals.sandiegozoo.org/regions/north-america

GLOSSARY

algae (AL-jee)—Simple plants that do not have roots, stems, leaves, or flowers. They generally live in water, in large groups.

amphibians (am-FIH-bee-anz)—Group of cold-blooded animals that live both in water and on land.

arctic (ARK-tik)—Very cold areas near Earth's north and south poles.

biome (BY-ohm)—Any major region that has a specific climate and supports specific animals and plants.

burrow (BUR-oh)—To dig a hole or tunnel in the ground.

migration (my-GRAY-shun)—When an animal moves from one place to another, usually for better weather.

mollusks (MAH-luxz)—Group of animals that have soft bodies, often covered by shells. For example, oysters.

resplendent (re-SPLEN-dent)—Shining or glowing.

venom (VEN-um)—Poison inserted into the body instead of eaten.

PHOTO CREDITS

Cover—Denali National Park and Preserve; inside front cover—Shutterstock.com/ruboart; p. 1—Tambako the Jaguar; pp. 2-3—Sheila Sund; p. 2 (world map)—Shutterstock.com/Maxger; p. 4 (gila)—Shutterstock.com/Nick Fox; pp. 4-5—Shutterstock.com/Vaclav Sebek; pp. 6-7—Tupulak; pp. 8-9—Shutterstock.com/outdoorsman; p. 9 (coyote)—NPS.gov; pp. 10-11—USFWS Midwest; pp. 12-13—Chris Parker; p. 15 (grizzly)—Gregory Smith; p. 17 (inset)—Shutterstock.com/karenfoleyphotography; pp. 18-19—Shutterstock.com/Harry Collins Photography; p. 21 (inset)—Shutterstock.com/Deborah Ferrin; pp. 22-23—Shutterstock.com/konradrza; p. 23 (cottonmouth)—LtShears; pp. 24-25—Shutterstock.com/Petr Salinger; p. 25 (monarch)—DocentJoyce; p. 26 (lobster)—Steven Johnson; pp. 26-27—Shutterstock.com/Yarrrrrbright; p. 27 (crab)—Jarek Tuszynski; pp. 28-29—Shutterstock.com/Jen DeVos; inside back cover—Shutterstock.com/ruboart. All other photos—Public Domain. Every measure has been taken to find all copyright holders of material used in this book. In the event any mistakes or omissions have happened within, attempts to correct them will be made in future editions of the book.

ABOUT THE AUTHOR

Amie Jane Leavitt graduated from Brigham Young University and is an accomplished author, researcher, and photographer. She has written more than 60 books for kids, contributed to online and print media, and worked as a consultant, writer, and editor for numerous educational publishing and assessment companies. To check out a listing of Amie's current projects and published works, visit her website at www.amiejaneleavitt.com.

© 2024 by Curious Fox Books™, an imprint of Fox Chapel Publishing Company, Inc., 903 Square Street, Mount Joy, PA 17552.

Awesome Animals of North America is a revision of *The Animals of North America*, published in 2017 by Purple Toad Publishing, Inc. Reproduction of its contents is strictly prohibited without written permission from the rights holder.

Paperback ISBN 979-8-89094-109-1
Hardcover ISBN 978-8-89094-110-7

Library of Congress Control Number: 2024932971

To learn more about the other great books from Fox Chapel Publishing, or to find a retailer near you, call toll-free 800-457-9112 or visit us at *www.FoxChapelPublishing.com*.

We are always looking for talented authors. To submit an idea, please send a brief inquiry to acquisitions@foxchapelpublishing.com.

Fox Chapel Publishing makes every effort to use environmentally friendly paper for printing.

Printed in China